DK

STAR WARS® BLUEPRINTS

REBEL  EDITION

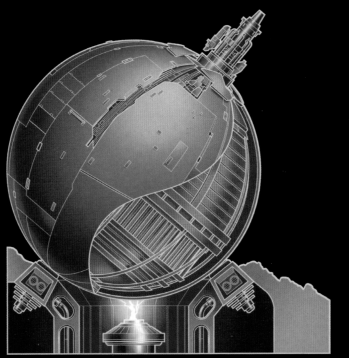

Illustrated by
CHRIS TREVAS and CHRIS REIFF

Written by RYDER WINDHAM

Incom T-65
X-wing

X-wing starfighters first flew against the Empire in the year prior to the Battle of Yavin, when the X-wing's Incom Corporation design team defected to the Alliance. Arhul Narra, a Clone Wars veteran, became the commander of the Rebel starfighter group Renegade Flight, which was named after the courageous Incom defectors. Following the Battle of Yavin, Commander Narra co-founded the elite starfighter unit Rogue Squadron with Luke Skywalker and Wedge Antilles. Although Rogue Squadron also flew T-47 airspeeders and Z-95 headhunters, it remains primarily identified by T-65 X-wings.

THE BATTLE OF YAVIN

Imperial turbolaser defenses were too ponderous to stop swift X-wings from traveling into the Death Star's trenches. Rebel pilots had to slow their speed to allow their targeting computers to aim for the two-meter (6.5-feet)-wide thermal exhaust port located in the polar trench. Luke Skywalker eschewed his computer and used the Force to find his target.

ON DAGOBAH

Seeking the Jedi Master Yoda, Luke Skywalker flew his X-wing to Dagobah, a remote, storm-shrouded world of swamps and overgrown trees. The X-wing's structural integrity enabled Luke to survive a crash-landing in a back-water bog. The astromech droid R2-D2 removed mud and muck from the ship's systems to ensure it remained flightworthy.

A NEW DEATH STAR

After the Alliance learned that the Empire was constructing a new Death Star in the Endor system, Rebel pilot Wedge Antilles led a starfighter division into the battle station's reactor core. Antilles had previously flown an X-wing at the Battle of Yavin and a snowspeeder at the Battle of Hoth. With Lando Calrissian, he is credited with destroying the second Death Star.

Starfighter

T-65 X-wing

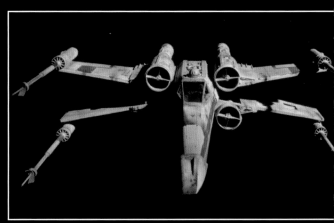

The T-65 starfighter originated as a top-secret project of the Incom Corporation. Incom was also the manufacturer of the fighter's Clone Wars predecessor, the Aggressive ReConnassiance-170 (ARC-170), which also had moveable cannon-tipped wings. After the Empire nationalized Incom, courageous technicians and suppliers defected to the Rebellion, taking the T-65 prototypes with them. Informally referred to as a "snub fighter" by its pilots, the T-65 was dubbed "X-wing" because of the configuration it assumes during combat —when its double-layered, cannon-tipped Strike foils (S-foils) fully extend to an "X" formation to increase their range of fire. The T-65 combines great speed with super maneuverability while carrying heavy firepower. After the Rebel hero Luke Skywalker piloted his T-65 to destroy the Empire's Death Star battle station at the historic Battle of Yavin, the X-wing became a symbol of the Rebel Alliance.

TARGETING COMPUTER AND SENSORS

The T-65 utilizes a Fabritech ANq 3.6 tracking computer, an IN-344-B "Sightline" holographic imaging system, and a sensor array to locate and display tactical imagery on a targeting scope. A targeting computer screen mask extends on a mechanical arm to assist the pilot with precise firing data during bombing runs. The T-65's sensor array consists of a Fabritech ANS-5d "lock track" full spectrum transceiver, a Melihat "multi-imager" dedicated energy receptor, and a Tana Ire electrophoto receptor. A Fabritech k-blakan mini sensor provides the pilot with a view of the ship's rear arc. The sensor array feeds data to the ANq 3.6, which can track up to 1,000 moving sublight objects, acquire 20 possible targets, and can be programmed for extra sensitivity to 120 specific sensor signatures. The tracking computer has a success rate of 98.7 percent.

(1) Sensor window   (3) Targeting computer
(2) Sensor computer

Targeting scope

MG7-A PROTON TORPEDO

(4) Warhead   (5) Guidance gyro   (6) Power s

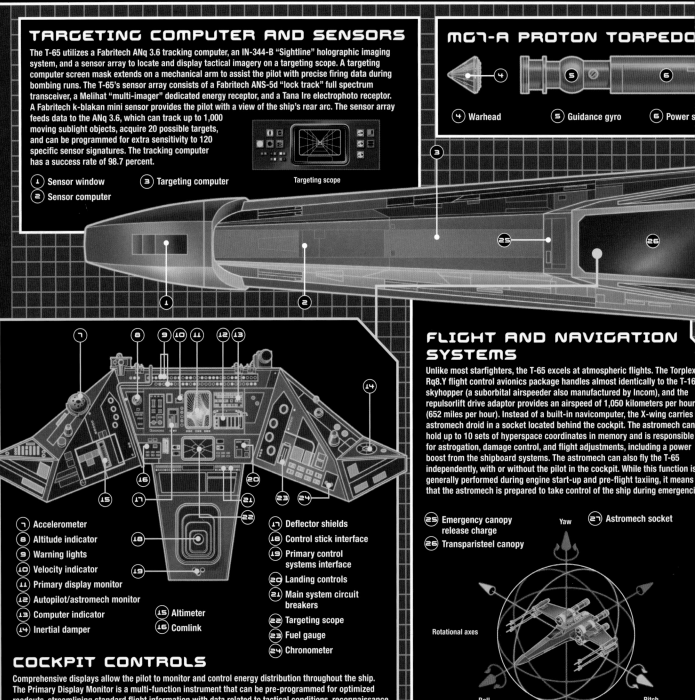

FLIGHT AND NAVIGATION SYSTEMS

Unlike most starfighters, the T-65 excels at atmospheric flights. The Torplex Rq8.Y flight control avionics package handles almost identically to the T-16 skyhopper (a suborbital airspeeder also manufactured by Incom), and the repulsorlift drive adaptor provides an airspeed of 1,050 kilometers per hour (652 miles per hour). Instead of a built-in navicomputer, the X-wing carries astromech droid in a socket located behind the cockpit. The astromech can hold up to 10 sets of hyperspace coordinates in memory and is responsible for astrogation, damage control, and flight adjustments, including a power boost from the shipboard systems. The astromech can also fly the T-65 independently, with or without the pilot in the cockpit. While this function is generally performed during engine start-up and pre-flight taxiing, it means that the astromech is prepared to take control of the ship during emergenci

(25) Emergency canopy release charge   Yaw   (27) Astromech socket
(26) Transparisteel canopy

Rotational axes

Roll   Pitch

COCKPIT CONTROLS

(7) Accelerometer
(8) Altitude indicator
(9) Warning lights
(10) Velocity indicator
(11) Primary display monitor
(12) Autopilot/astromech monitor
(13) Computer indicator
(14) Inertial damper
(15) Altimeter
(16) Comlink
(17) Deflector shields
(18) Control stick interface
(19) Primary control systems interface
(20) Landing controls
(21) Main system circuit breakers
(22) Targeting scope
(23) Fuel gauge
(24) Chronometer

Comprehensive displays allow the pilot to monitor and control energy distribution throughout the ship. The Primary Display Monitor is a multi-function instrument that can be pre-programmed for optimized readouts, streamlining standard flight information with data related to tactical conditions, reconnaissance, and communications. The autopilot/astromech monitor provides data for the astromech's Systems and serves as a teletext translator, enabling the pilot to converse with the astromech. Because the X-wing's controls are so similar to those in the T-16 skyhopper, Rebel pilots are often initially trained in the relatively inexpensive T-16.

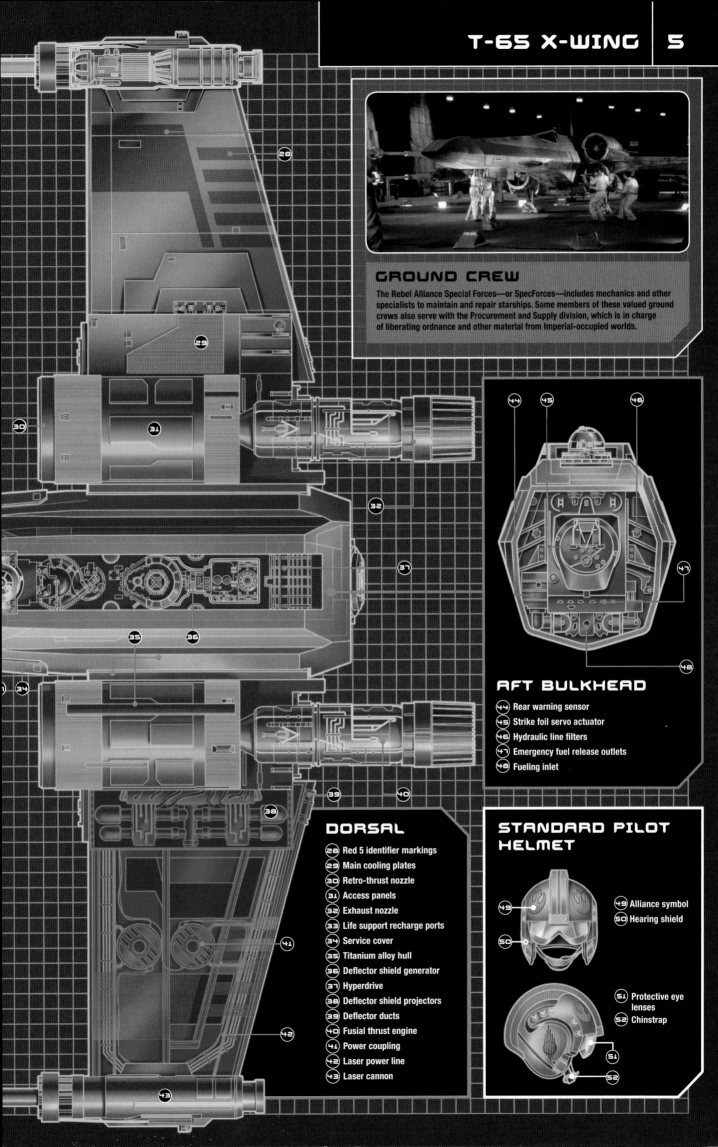

GROUND CREW

The Rebel Alliance Special Forces—or SpecForces—includes mechanics and other specialists to maintain and repair starships. Some members of these valued ground crews also serve with the Procurement and Supply division, which is in charge of liberating ordnance and other material from Imperial-occupied worlds.

AFT BULKHEAD

44 Rear warning sensor
45 Strike foil servo actuator
46 Hydraulic line filters
47 Emergency fuel release outlets
48 Fueling inlet

DORSAL

28 Red 5 identifier markings
29 Main cooling plates
30 Retro-thrust nozzle
31 Access panels
32 Exhaust nozzle
33 Life support recharge ports
34 Service cover
35 Titanium alloy hull
36 Deflector shield generator
37 Hyperdrive
38 Deflector shield projectors
39 Deflector ducts
40 Fusial thrust engine
41 Power coupling
42 Laser power line
43 Laser cannon

STANDARD PILOT HELMET

49 Alliance symbol
50 Hearing shield

51 Protective eye lenses
52 Chinstrap

OFFENSIVE SYSTEMS

The T-65's four forward-firing Taim & Bak KX9 laser cannons are engineered to generate maximum destructive power; the length of the cannons means longer range for its lasers. When the S-foils split into attack position, the lasers target a specific "zero" point, typically half a kilometer (a third of a mile) away. The cannons can be set for single fire (each cannon fires individually), dual fire (starboard and port cannons fire alternately), or quad fire (all four cannons fire simultaneously). For even longer range targeting, the T-65 has two Krupx MG7 proton torpedo launchers. Each launcher fires from a three-torpedo magazine for a total payload of six warheads. MG7-A torpedoes are focused nuclear explosives used for critical target destruction or for punching through a target's ray shielding. The torpedo launchers are removed from X-wing recon fighters and replaced with high-gain long-range sensors, processors, and high-speed hypertransceivers. All T-65s also use an offensive defense: A Bertriak "Screamer" sensor jammer that can block sensors on enemy starfighters and thwart homing warheads.

- 53 Laser generator
- 54 Laser cooling sleeve
- 55 Magnetic flashback suppressors
- 56 Laser tip
- 57 Cockpit
- 58 Nose cone
- 59 Torpedo launchers
- 60 Cargo bay door
- 61 Strike foils—stowed (Primary cruise mode)
- 62 Strike foils—deployed (Primary attack mode)

Laser Cannon

SUBLIGHT ENGINES

The X-wing's remarkable maneuverability is attributed to three factors. The first is differential thrust from its four Incom 4L4 fusial ion engines, which allow the fighter to quickly adjust its trajectory. Second, each of the four retro-thrusters has high-mass electromagnetic gyros that help swing the ship in tight curves. Third, precise bursts of retro-thrust fire forward through the turbine nozzles for increased control—an absolute necessity in combat.

- 63 Turbo generator
- 64 Turbo impeller
- 65 Fission chamber
- 66 Alluvial damper
- 67 Reactant injector
- 68 Ground power input
- 69 Power converter
- 70 Power surge vent
- 71 Stabilizer
- 72 Hyperdrive motivator
- 73 Electromagnetic gyros
- 74 Cooling vanes

ASTROMEC DROIDS

Most Rebel starfighters utili astromech droids for in-flig repairs and navigation. X-w are designed to accommoda Industrial Automaton's succ R-series of droids, including R5 units, which are hoisted X-wing's astromech socket Rebel pilots develop affiniti their droids and starfighters even regard the droids as f

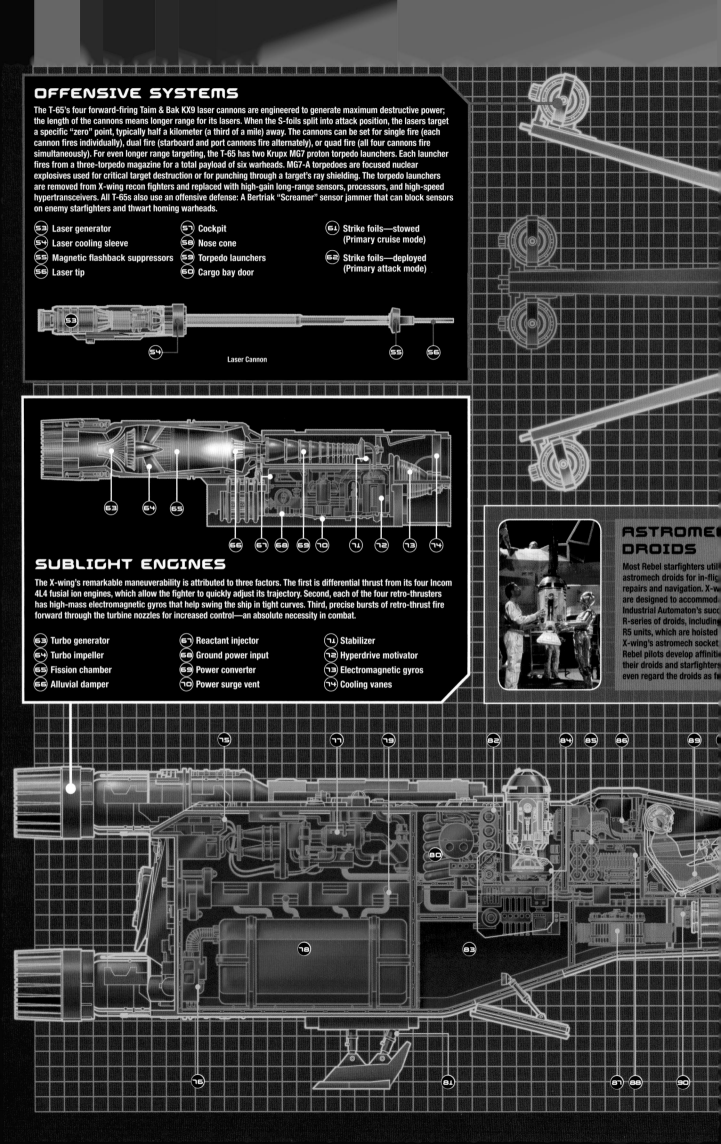

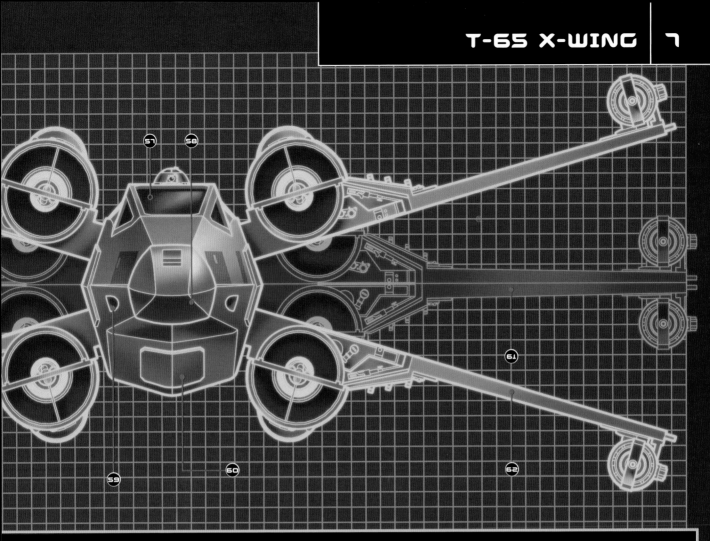

STARBOARD

The X-wing's hull is composed of hardened titanium armor alloy, reinforced with the expensive and high-strength alloy sedrellium. A military-grade deflector shield generator produces basic shield matrices through a catalyzation process and then feeds deflector ducts on the fighter's surface and Chempat deflector shield projectors for starboard and port shields. A compact life-support system consists of compressors, temperature regulators, and oxygen scrubbing filters. The ship holds enough oxygen, fuel, and power for a week of non-combat operations. Acceleration compensators protect the pilot from deadly G-forces during high-speed maneuvers. Unlike Imperial starfighters, the X-wing allows for an emergency bail out, with separator charges to blast the cockpit canopy free, and a Guidenhauser ejection seat to launch the pilot clear from the fighter. A separate ejector launches the astromech unit from its socket. The cargo compartment—with a capacity of two cubic meters (71 cubic feet) and rated for 110 kilograms (242 pounds)—is generally used to hold survival and repair gear.

75 Hyperdrive
76 Fuel pump
77 Main cooling system
78 Fuel tank
79 Fuel lines
80 Power generator
81 Landing gear
82 Power converters
83 Cargo bay
84 Droid lift platform
85 Life support system
86 Targeting computer subsystem

87 Acceleration compensator
88 Atmospheric scrubbers
89 Ejection system
90 Torpedo sequencing servo
91 Primary control systems
92 Proton torpedo
93 Pitch and roll control pedals
94 Avionics sub-processor
95 Flight computer
96 Repulsorlift
97 Landing gear door
98 Subspace radio

99 Communications antenna
100 Sensor computer
101 Hydraulic lines
102 Primary sensor array
103 Enemy sensor jammer unit
104 Nose cone
105 Lantern
106 Emergency transmitter
107 Toolbox
108 Portable generator
109 Emergency supplies and rations
110 Emergency shelter

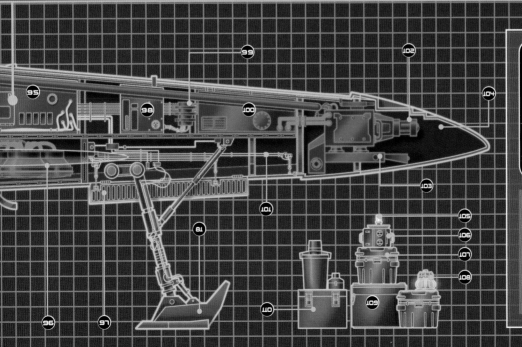

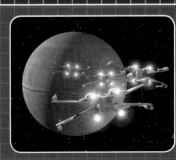

S-FOILS

Echoing the unfolding split transverse wings of the Incom/Subpro ARC-170 starfighter used by Republic forces during the Clone Wars, the X-wing's Strike foils provide better weapons coverage and also present a smaller target, whether the wings are closed for atmospheric flights or deployed for combat.

Since its introduction during the Clone Wars, the BTL Y-wing starfighter has proven its worth in countless battles throughout the galaxy. It has the distinction of being the Rebellion's first hyperdrive-equipped fighter, which allowed the earliest group of Rebel pilots to travel through hyperspace to a distant sector, hit their targets, and then escape back into hyperspace before Imperial forces could react. Because Y-wings are affordable and easy to obtain and modify, it comes as no surprise that there are far more Y-wings than any other single craft in the Rebel fleet.

THE CLONE WARS

During the Clone Wars, the Jedi Knight Anakin Skywalker personally trained Shadow Squadron to fly their new BTL-B Y-wing starfighters and led them on a rescue mission to the Abregado system. Anakin's Padawan, Ahsoka Tano, served as his gunner in the fighter's bubble turret, while the astromech socket was occupied by the plucky R2-D2.

BATTLE OF YAVIN

At the Battle of Yavin, three Rebel pilots of Gold Squadron—Jon Vander (Gold Leader), Tiree (Gold Two), and Davish "Pops" Krail (Gold Five)—flew their Y-wings in the first bombing run into the Death Star's trench. Meanwhile, Keyan Farlander (Gold Seven) provided tactical support and held off enemy TIE fighters. Farlander was his squadron's only survivor.

BATTLE OF ENDOR

Until the advent of the B-wing starfighter, the Y-wing was the only attack craft in the Rebel fleet that carried an ion cannon system. Despite the X-wing and A-wing being faster and more maneuverable, and the B-wing having greater firepower, Rebel pilot Horton Salm did not hesitate to fly his Y-wing into the second Death Star at the Battle of Endor.

Starfighter

BTL Y-wing

Developed by Koensayr during the early stages of the Clone Wars, the original Y-wing starfighter was the BTL-B bomber, a double-seater craft with a forward-facing pilot and a tailgunner in a rotating bubble turret. Koensayr has produced many variations, all with the same basic configuration of a wedge-shaped cockpit module trailed by a reinforced central spar that houses an astromech socket. The central spar is connected to a cross-spar and each end of the cross-spar is secured to a long pylon that houses a sublight and hyperdrive engine. Early in the Galactic Civil War, the Y-wing was the most easily available starfighter to the Rebel Alliance. Most Y-wing fighters have been supplanted by the more maneuverable and powerful X-wing for combat missions, but the Alliance continues to use stripped-down, single-seat BTL-A4s for escort duty, reconnaissance, light bombing runs, and surgical strikes.

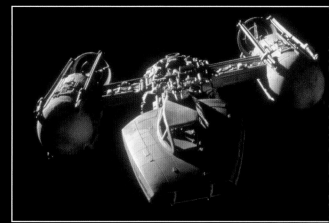

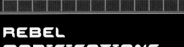

REBEL MODIFICATIONS

Alliance technicians removed much of the Y-wing's armor to reduce weight and shortened the engine support pylons for greater maneuverability in close combat. Surplus Y-wing armor is refitted for other Alliance ships, notably the modified T-47 snowspeeder. Technicians also replaced the Y-wing's original torpedo magazines with lighter and more compact four-torpedo magazines that feed into a pair of Arakyd FlexTube proton torpedo launchers. A fuel recycling system that is extremely efficient for long-range missions is kept in place on courier configurations like the BTL-S3, but it is removed from bombers, as the heavy system can actually inhibit overall performance, especially during quick hit-and-run missions.

1. Reinforced tail
2. Fuel reclamator
3. Electromagnetic gyro filter
4. Backup batteries
5. Secondary life support
6. Fresh water tanks
7. Proton torpedo launch racks
8. Power coupling
9. Vectral ring
10. Thrust vectrals
11. Exhaust nozzle
12. Turbo modifications

DORSAL

The original BTL-B Y-wing's fuselage and engines were fully covered by streamlined armored plating and were equipped with twin proton torpedo launchers with magazines that held six torpedoes each.

13. Composite sensor dome
14. Main power cell
15. Wing repulsorlift
16. Cooling intakes
17. Rear sensor
18. Deflector shield generator
19. Hyperdrive tachyon exhaust
20. Hyperdrive sequencer
21. Deflector shield projectors
22. Main coolant pump
23. Titanium-reinforced Alusteel hull
24. Life support equipment

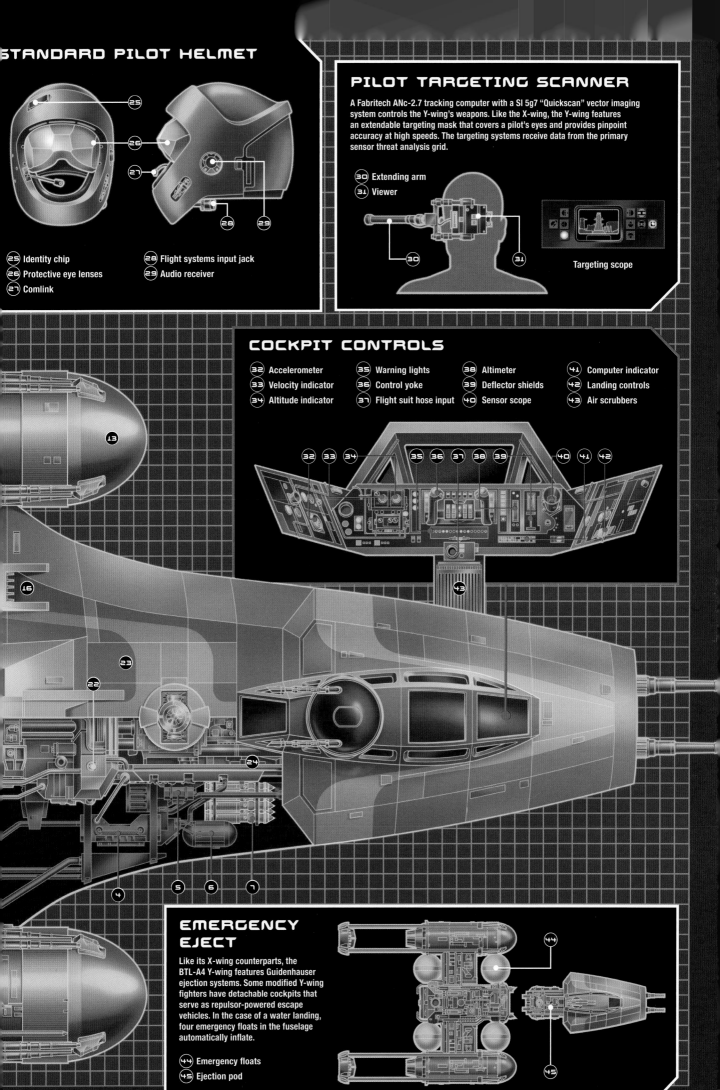

STANDARD PILOT HELMET

25 Identity chip
26 Protective eye lenses
27 Comlink
28 Flight systems input jack
29 Audio receiver

PILOT TARGETING SCANNER

A Fabritech ANc-2.7 tracking computer with a SI 5g7 "Quickscan" vector imaging system controls the Y-wing's weapons. Like the X-wing, the Y-wing features an extendable targeting mask that covers a pilot's eyes and provides pinpoint accuracy at high speeds. The targeting systems receive data from the primary sensor threat analysis grid.

30 Extending arm
31 Viewer

Targeting scope

COCKPIT CONTROLS

32 Accelerometer
33 Velocity indicator
34 Altitude indicator
35 Warning lights
36 Control yoke
37 Flight suit hose input
38 Altimeter
39 Deflector shields
40 Sensor scope
41 Computer indicator
42 Landing controls
43 Air scrubbers

EMERGENCY EJECT

Like its X-wing counterparts, the BTL-A4 Y-wing features Guidenhauser ejection systems. Some modified Y-wing fighters have detachable cockpits that serve as repulsor-powered escape vehicles. In the case of a water landing, four emergency floats in the fuselage automatically inflate.

44 Emergency floats
45 Ejection pod

KEYAN FARLANDER

Like Luke Skywalker, Keyan "Lucky" Farlander learned how to fly using a T-16 skyhopper. A native of the agriworld Agamar, he joined a resistance movement against the Empire after Imperial forces destroyed his hometown of Tondatha. He subsequently joined the Rebel Alliance, became a starfighter pilot, and participated in numerous rescue missions as well as raids on Imperial convoys. He flew a Y-wing at the Battle of Yavin and was among the first pilots to fly a B-wing in combat.

PROTON TORPEDO WARHEAD

First used in the Clone Wars, proton torpedoes are high-speed projectile weapons that release a wave of high-energy proton particles on impact. The Krupx MG7 proton torpedo features guidance computers and is generally used to soften targets for strafing runs, but it can also take out key targets such as engines and shield generators.

- 46 Propellant cylinder
- 47 Energy envelope projector
- 48 Ignition charge
- 49 Homing sensor

ORIGINAL TURRET

The BTL-B Y-wing came equipped with a transparisteel bubble turret that rotated 360 degrees. Although enclosed turrets offer greater protection from enemy fire, vintage bubbles allow clear, unobstructed views of surrounding space and a greater field of fire. While some Rebel gunners maintain that the bubble's advantages make it worth the risk, most bubbles have been recycled for use on Rebel bases and strongholds.

Targeting Screen

STARBOARD

Twin Koensayr R200 ion fission engines propel the Y-wing in real space, and each ion fission engine nacelle is topped with sophisticated sensor arrays. In atmospheric flights, these engines work in conjunction with recessed repulsorlift generators to attain speeds of 1,000 kilometers (620 miles) per hour. Chempat shield projectors cover the Y-wing with defensive energy. The Koensayr R300-H hyperdrive motivator yields a Class One performance on standard astrogation routes. Because the Y-wing runs very hot for a ship of its size, a complex cooling system extends throughout the ship, and requires maintenance after every flight. Alliance technicians—aggravated by the need to remove hull panels to access machinery for every maintenance check— eventually chose to increase shield power and leave most of the armor off.

- 50 Support pylons
- 51 Heavy ion jet turbines
- 52 Landing gear
- 53 Ion turbo injector
- 54 Ion fission reactor
- 55 Fuel accelerator
- 56 Pulse electromagnets
- 57 Long-range targeting sensor array
- 58 Heat vents
- 59 Astromech droid
- 60 Ship-to-ship photonic comm system
- 61 Neck repulsorlift
- 62 Acceleration compensator
- 63 Laser generator heat sink
- 64 Coolant coils
- 65 Main laser coolant p...
- 66 Torpedo launch tube
- 67 Forward laser coolar...
- 68 Harmonic vibration d...
- 69 Harmonic field senso...
- 70 Laser tip

THRUST VECTORING

The Y-wing's maneuverability is credited to two thruster control jets in the aft-face of the central spar. Disk-vectrals set in the end of the engine nacelles to redirect thrust provide additional agility.

- 71 Vectral ring
- 72 Thrust vectrals

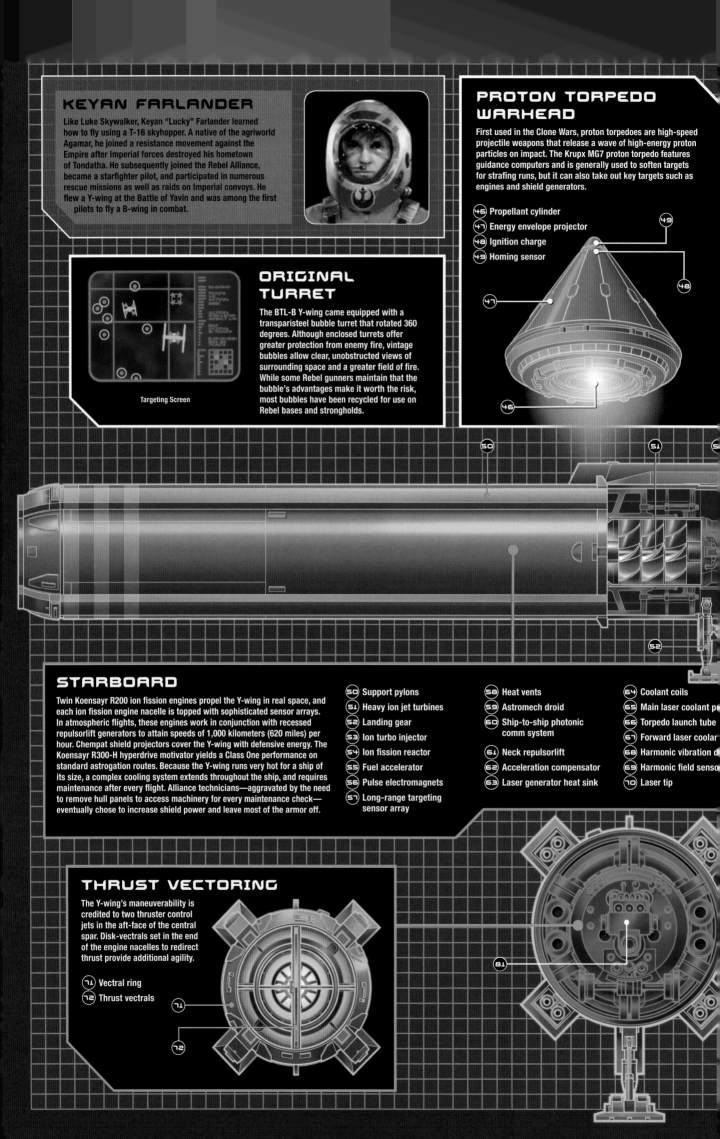

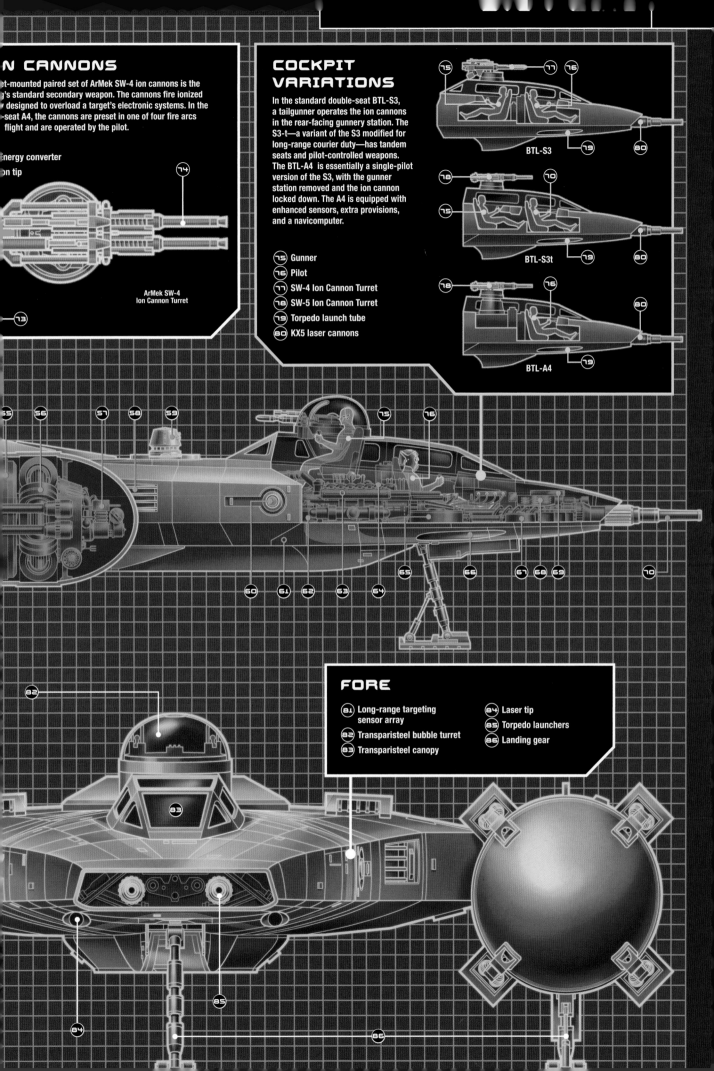

N CANNONS

t-mounted paired set of ArMek SW-4 ion cannons is the
g's standard secondary weapon. The cannons fire ionized
y designed to overload a target's electronic systems. In the
-seat A4, the cannons are preset in one of four fire arcs
flight and are operated by the pilot.

nergy converter

n tip

ArMek SW-4
Ion Cannon Turret

COCKPIT VARIATIONS

In the standard double-seat BTL-S3,
a tailgunner operates the ion cannons
in the rear-facing gunnery station. The
S3-t—a variant of the S3 modified for
long-range courier duty—has tandem
seats and pilot-controlled weapons.
The BTL-A4 is essentially a single-pilot
version of the S3, with the gunner
station removed and the ion cannon
locked down. The A4 is equipped with
enhanced sensors, extra provisions,
and a navicomputer.

75 Gunner
16 Pilot
77 SW-4 Ion Cannon Turret
78 SW-5 Ion Cannon Turret
79 Torpedo launch tube
80 KX5 laser cannons

BTL-S3

BTL-S3t

BTL-A4

FORE

81 Long-range targeting
sensor array
82 Transparisteel bubble turret
83 Transparisteel canopy

84 Laser tip
85 Torpedo launchers
86 Landing gear

Rebel
Blockade

The Corellian Engineering Corvette CR90 is the starship of choice for everyone from respectable diplomats to notorious pirates. More than a decade before the Clone Wars, Queen Mazicia Organa of the planet Alderaan commissioned the *Star of Alderaan* to serve as a consular vessel for Senator Agrippa Aldrete. After the queen's son, Bail Organa, ascended to Viceroy and became a Senatorial representative, he renamed the ship the *Tantive IV* in tribute to visiting ambassadors from the Tantive system. It served House Organa for 30 years until its capture by the Empire, after which Darth Vader ordered it be destroyed.

ALDERAAN

The Corvette's legacy as a diplomatic vessel was cemented during a mission to Toydaria that eventually led to the opening up of talks between the neutral planet and the Republic. Bail Organa used the CR70 *Sundered Heart*, which was in dry dock at the end of the Clone Wars, when he adopted an infant girl named Leia and brought her to Alderaan.

CAPTURED

Nineteen years after her adoption, Leia Organa was a Senator as well as a member of the Rebel Alliance. Having intercepted plans for an Imperial superweapon, she raced to the planet Tatooine in the *Tantive IV*. An Imperial Star Destroyer, under the command of Darth Vader, disabled Leia's ship and snared it with a powerful tractor beam.

SECRET PLANS

After Imperial forces seized the *Tantive IV*, Leia momentarily evaded stormtroopers in a dimly illuminated subhallway linking the port airlock to the escape pod access tunnel. Knowing her capture was imminent, she entrusted astromech droid R2-D2 to deliver a message and the plans for the superweapon to Obi-Wan Kenobi on Tatooine.

Runner

Rebel Blockade Runner

Of all the easily modifiable starships manufactured by Corellian Engineering Corporation (CEC), the Corellian Corvette is considered the most versatile. Its uses include cargo ship, passenger carrier, troop transport, and light escort vehicle. Original stock models did not include weapons, but came with modular weapons emplacements for as many as eight turbolasers, six laser cannons, and four ion cannons. During the Galactic Civil War, the Corvettes were so strongly associated with the Rebel Alliance—who used them to evade Imperial capture—that they became commonly referred to as Rebel Blockade Runners. The CR90 Corvette *Tantive IV* was one of several Corvettes registered to the Royal House of Alderaan.

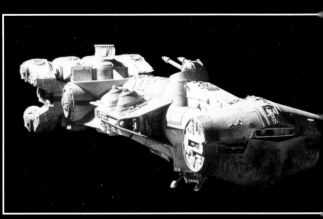

COCKPIT MODULE

1. Cockpit
2. Shield generator
3. Navigation/tactical planning
4. Forward elevator
5. Computer power substation
6. Forward airlock docking hatch
7. Cockpit viewport
8. Automated docking signal receiver
9. Defensive field projector
10. Captain's quarters

DORSAL

11. Officer's quarters
12. Power distribution control
13. Environmental control
14. Operations forum
15. Conference chamber
16. Emergency power generators
17. Escape pod access tunnel
18. Tech station
19. Mid-ship elevator
20. Main corridor
21. Engine systems monitoring
22. Equipment storage
23. Main reactor
24. Pressurized fuel cell
25. Hyperdrive generator
26. Heat exhaust panel
27. Power feed manifold
28. Hyperdrive tachyon exhaust
29. Ion pre-cycle impellers
30. Ion accelerator
31. Fuel pre-cycler
32. Ion turbine
33. Turbo injectors
34. Electromagnetic panels
35. Thrust nozzles

ESCAPE PODS

ur armored lifeboats double as long-range Taim & Bak laser rrets. Each lifeboat seats up to 12 passengers, including a lot/gunner who can either control the flight and weapons stems or allow them to operate automatically. Chemical ckets propel the pods across space, while a flight computer ots a course away from danger. The Corvette also carries ght six-being escape pods. To protect passengers from ury, a padded g-couch rings the interior, which contains mergency supplies and food rations.

36 Laser turret
37 Access ladder
38 Maneuvering jets
39 Boarding hatch
40 Repulsor soft-landing coils
41 Gravity/antigravity ring
42 Control console

43 Emergency beacon
44 Escape thrusters
45 Fuel cells
46 Life support system
47 Emergency supplies
48 Viewport
49 Egress hatch

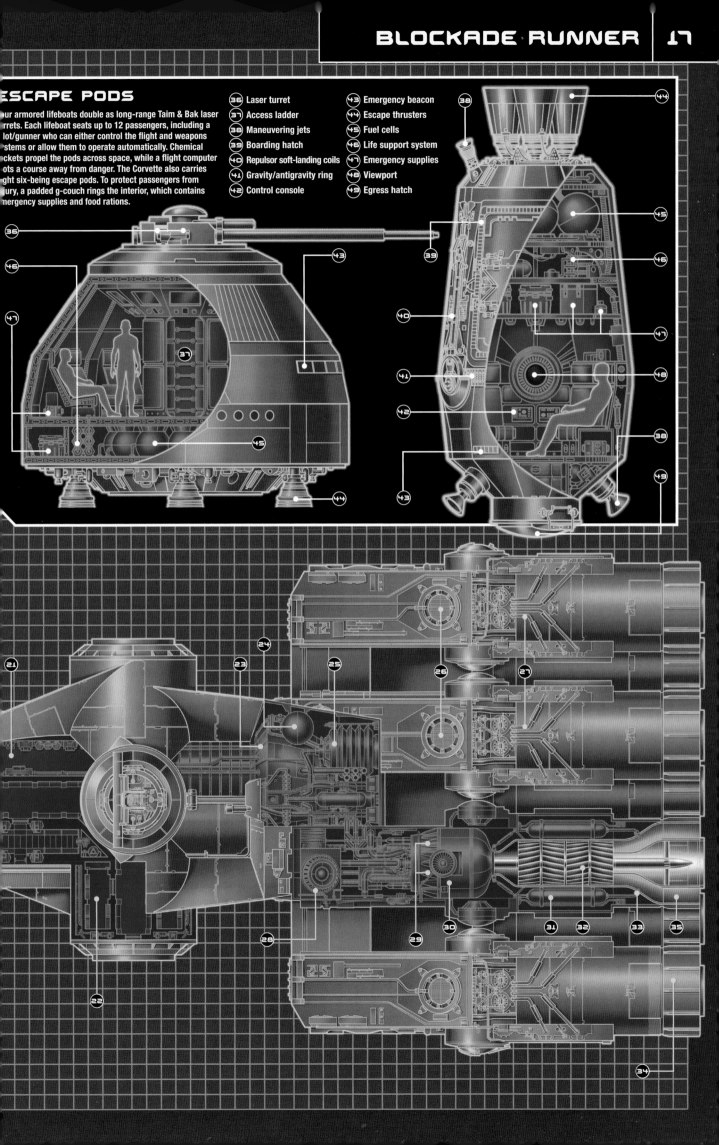

PORT

50 Landing gear
51 Dual turbolasers
52 Added armor plate
53 Stateroom suite
54 Long-range laser turret
55 High-capacity escape pods
56 Escape pods
57 Mid-ship elevator
58 Maintenance shaft
59 Hangar/cargo bay
60 Atmosphere tanks
61 Airlock doorway
62 Primary sensor array
63 Boarding ramp
64 Comm and sensor array (retracted)

EMERGENCY EVACUATION

Although each escape pod's shipboard systems are automated to guide and deliver the craft to the optimum landing point, a simple piloting station provides access to the sensor, communication, and flight control systems. After Darth Vader captured Rebel leader Princess Leia Organa on the *Tantive IV*, the droids R2-D2 and C-3PO made a hasty getaway in an unarmed escape pod to the sand planet Tatooine.

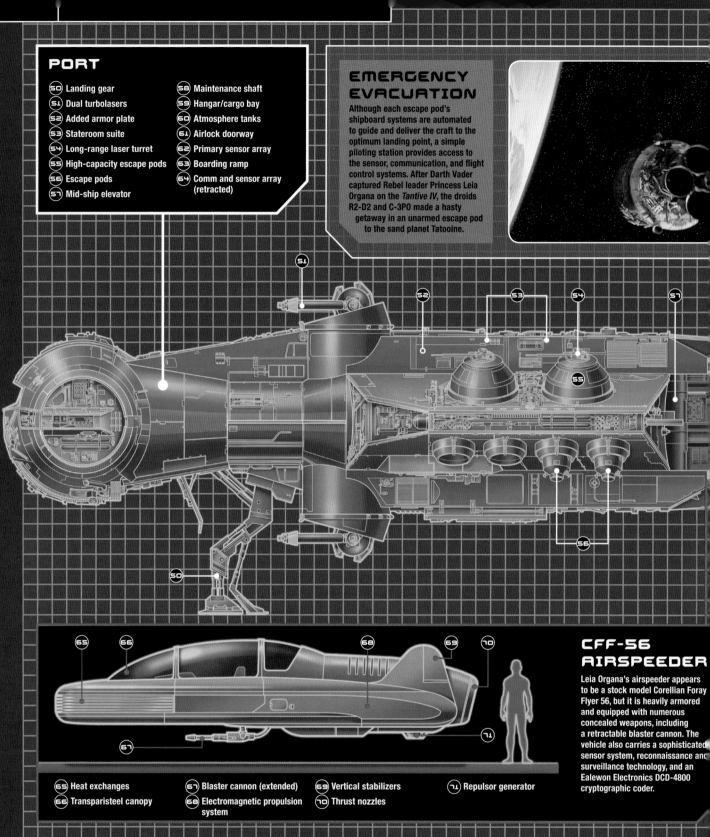

CFF-56 AIRSPEEDER

Leia Organa's airspeeder appears to be a stock model Corellian Foray Flyer 56, but it is heavily armored and equipped with numerous concealed weapons, including a retractable blaster cannon. The vehicle also carries a sophisticated sensor system, reconnaissance and surveillance technology, and an Ealewon Electronics DCD-4800 cryptographic coder.

65 Heat exchanges
66 Transparisteel canopy
67 Blaster cannon (extended)
68 Electromagnetic propulsion system
69 Vertical stabilizers
70 Thrust nozzles
71 Repulsor generator

CR70 SUNDERED HEART

The CR70 Corvette is the predecessor to the more widely used CR90 Corvette. A smaller vessel, the CR70 saw frequent use in diplomatic and transport roles. Unarmed and boasting additional escape pods, it was among the most popular civilian transports in the galaxy prior to the rise of the Empire. It had been in service for many years before the outbreak of the Clone Wars and, though it was considered an older design, it was still in production in large quantities in the years prior to the Battle of Geonosis. The CR70 Corvette *Sundered Heart* was used by Bail Organa and the Royal House of Alderaan in the final days of the Clone Wars.

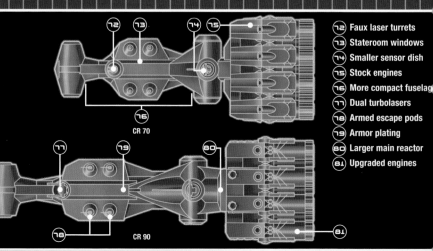

CR 70

CR 90

72 Faux laser turrets
73 Stateroom windows
74 Smaller sensor dish
75 Stock engines
76 More compact fuselage
77 Dual turbolasers
78 Armed escape pods
79 Armor plating
80 Larger main reactor
81 Upgraded engines

SENSOR ARRAY

[e] primary sensor array collects environmental and
[n]vigational data. Because the array is positioned on a
[fin] above the main reactor, damage to the array and fin
[n] cause vibrations that overload the reactor, which
[mu]st then be shut down, effectively crippling the ship.

- [a] **Rectenna**
- [a] **Active sensors**
- [a] **Passive sensors**

CONFERENCE ROOM

The Corvettes used by House Organa
feature a centrally located formal state
conference chamber that can seat over
a dozen people around a long table with
data-display and communications
consoles. It was in one such room that
Jedi Master Yoda, Obi-Wan Kenobi, and
Bail Organa conferred on the fate of
Padmé Amidala's twins, Luke and Leia.

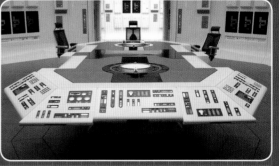

MAIN AIRLOCK

[For] docking with other ships or spaceport passage
[way]es, the Corvette's primary airlock consists of a
[pre]ssurized chamber that allows beings safe entrance
[and] exit without exposure to lethal atmospheres or the
[va]cuum of space. The airlock is secured by Locris
[Sy]ndicates MLC-50 magna locks. These are surface
[loc]king mechanisms that shape micro magnetic fields
[to] form almost molecular bonds between the armored
[hat]ch and hull. Despite the extra security, the airlock—
[lik]e any heavily shielded reinforcement—can be
[bre]ached by explosive firepower.

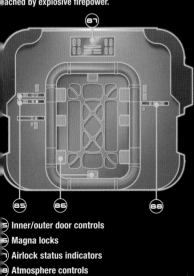

- [5] **Inner/outer door controls**
- [6] **Magna locks**
- [7] **Airlock status indicators**
- [8] **Atmosphere controls**

AFT

Before the rise of the Empire, CEC promoted the Corvette's evasive ability
as a selling point to members of the Galactic Senate. The Corvette has a
massive drive block of 11 ion turbine engines that enable it to easily outrun
most enemy ships. Electromagnetic panels at the end of each nozzle serve to
bend thrust streams and provide turning
force. The efficient sublight drive and
hyperjump calculator allow quick escapes
into hyperspace.

- [89] **Primary sensor array**
- [90] **Drive engines**
- [91] **Comm and sensor array**
- [92] **Thrust nozzles**

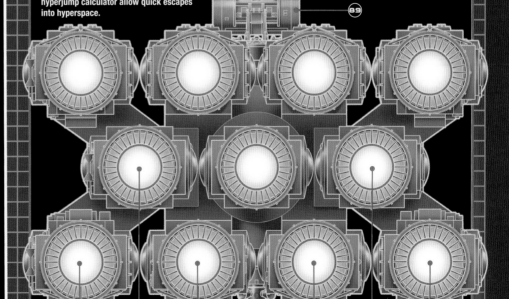

Rebel Weapons

Despite the Empire's effort to control the distribution of blaster weapons in numerous star systems, Rebel forces have had moderate success seizing blasters from manufacturers who hold contracts with the Empire. After Rebel privateers captured the design documents for the Imperial-intended Czerka 411 hold-out blaster, along with an entire factory run in transit to Coruscant, the Czerka 411 became a favorite of Rebellion espionage agents. Such acquisitions are not typical, but the Alliance is fortunate in that new enlisters often bring their own weapons, some of which—like Wookiee bowcasters—are unique to their owners.

DEFENDER SPORTING BLASTER

Like most sporting blaster pistols, Drearian Defense Conglomerate's Defender is typically personalized to provide an ideal shooting weight and aim for its wielder. Such low-powered pistols are generally used for target practice, self-defense, and small-game hunting. Rebel leader Leia Organa was an expert shot with her Defender, a gift from her father.

BLASTECH A280

Manufactured by the same company responsible for the Imperial-issue E-11 blaster rifle, the BlasTech A280 is a long-barreled, armor-piercing rifle. The A280 is based on the initial design of its predecessor, the DLT-20A. Both weapons are designated "Longblasters," designed and engineered for stopping long-range targets.

WOOKIEE BOWCASTER

A fusion of ancient weaponry and contemporary technology, Wookiee bowcasters are hand-built by Wookiee weaponsmiths and require great strength to operate. Rebel crossbowmen less physically powerful that the mighty Chewbacca use the Drolan Plasteel-manufactured repeating crossbow, which combines a bowcaster with a blaster rifle.

Rebel Weapons

Throughout the galaxy, the dominant weapons are ranged weapons that allow soldiers and hunters to strike a target from a safe distance. Although some civilizations continue to use relatively "primitive" projectile-firing weapons, the majority relies upon energy weapons. The most common energy weapons are blaster pistols and blaster rifles, generally referred to as blasters, which fire bolts of concentrated, coherent light that strike with a concussive impact. Most contemporary blasters either have built-in controls or can be modified to stun an opponent. The Empire's distribution restrictions on weapons prompt Rebel soldiers to arm themselves with stolen or outdated blasters, obtained by way of the black market, sympathetic supporters, or theft.

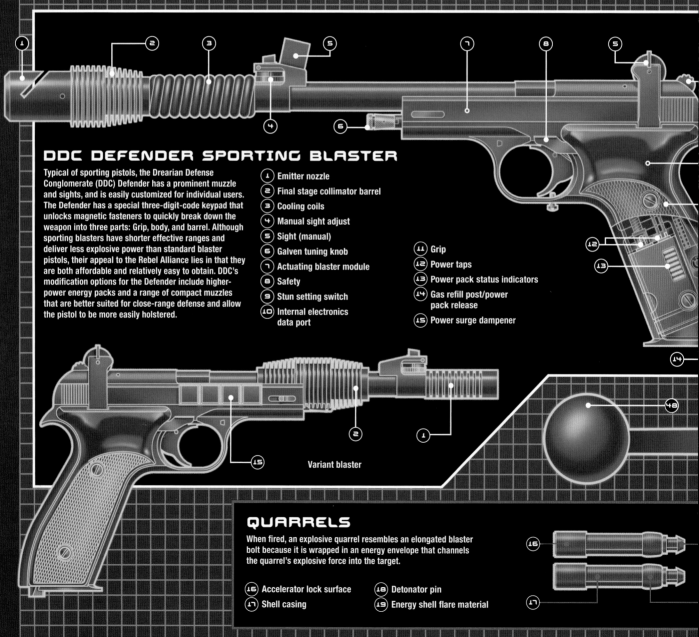

DDC DEFENDER SPORTING BLASTER

Typical of sporting pistols, the Drearian Defense Conglomerate (DDC) Defender has a prominent muzzle and sights, and is easily customized for individual users. The Defender has a special three-digit-code keypad that unlocks magnetic fasteners to quickly break down the weapon into three parts: Grip, body, and barrel. Although sporting blasters have shorter effective ranges and deliver less explosive power than standard blaster pistols, their appeal to the Rebel Alliance lies in that they are both affordable and relatively easy to obtain. DDC's modification options for the Defender include higher-power energy packs and a range of compact muzzles that are better suited for close-range defense and allow the pistol to be more easily holstered.

1. Emitter nozzle
2. Final stage collimator barrel
3. Cooling coils
4. Manual sight adjust
5. Sight (manual)
6. Galven tuning knob
7. Actuating blaster module
8. Safety
9. Stun setting switch
10. Internal electronics data port
11. Grip
12. Power taps
13. Power pack status indicators
14. Gas refill post/power pack release
15. Power surge dampener

Variant blaster

QUARRELS

When fired, an explosive quarrel resembles an elongated blaster bolt because it is wrapped in an energy envelope that channels the quarrel's explosive force into the target.

16. Accelerator lock surface
17. Shell casing
18. Detonator pin
19. Energy shell flare material

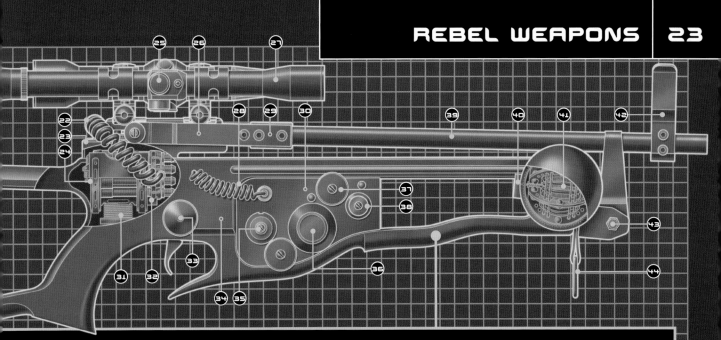

CHEWBACCA'S BOWCASTER

he traditional weapon of the Wookiees of Kashyyyk—the bowcaster r "laser crossbow"—is a ranged weapon that works on the principle magnetic acceleration. Twin spherical polarizers create alternating ositive and negative pulses to launch an explosive metal quarrel and enerate energy that envelops the quarrel as it travels through the aunch shaft. Typical bowcasters have an optimum range of 30 meters 8 feet) and a maximum range of 50 meters (164 feet), and can also e flash quarrels, smoke quarrels, sonic quarrels, and carved wooden olts. Not to be outgunned by Imperial stormtroopers, the Rebel hero hewbacca wields a machined bowcaster with an automatic ecocking system—a feature commonly found in the Wookiee infantry rces of the Clone Wars.

20 Stock
21 Heirloom bowstring
22 Polarity stabilizer crosslink
23 Breech cover
24 Ammo cartridge
25 Scope adjustment knob
26 Power pack release
27 Right stereo scope
28 Recharge power connect

29 Conduction chamber
30 Blaster gas chamber
31 Quarrel follower spring
32 Polarity stabilizer
33 Safety/fire mode select
34 Power pack
35 Barrel group release
36 Main power adjust
37 Gas cartridge release

38 Polarizer field balance
39 Launch shaft/barrel
40 Conducting rod
41 Magnetic acceleration coil
42 Manual front sight
43 Barrel group pivot
44 Carry-strap mount

STEREO-VIEW TARGETING

hewbacca the Wookiee modified a set of exotic electrobinocular scopes to work in njunction with a central, extendable military-grade low-light scope, which doubles as stereoscopic sight. All three scopes are linked by a compact computer that enhances e telescopic lenses up to 500 times magnification and automatically calculates range nd adjusts the bowcaster's collimating components. The left scope displays range data, e right scope displays power data, and imaging chips adjust and enhance visible light to low for observation in full daylight or near darkness. Ultrasonic beam emitters construct three-dimensional sound pattern of the target in the central scope. Despite his own odifications to the scopes, Chewbacca usually shoots by instinct and kinematics.

45 Left scope/Power display
46 Cental scope/Composite display
47 Right scope/Range display

PROD

Compared with traditional Wookiee bowcasters, which use tensile metal bowstrings to fire a variety of projectiles, Chewbacca's stringless automatic bowcaster is relatively limited in its power and accuracy but has a higher rate of fire. An expert shot, Chewbacca has adorned his weapons with an heirloom bowstring made from the vine of a kthysh plant.

48 Polarizer (2)
49 Conducting rod
50 Stereo targeting scopes
51 Launch shaft/barrel
52 Tension adjust
53 Carry strap mounts

BLASTECH DH-17 BLASTER RIFLE

Developed by BlasTech as a military-use sidearm, the DH-17 blaster rifle has been adopted by both the Imperial Navy and the Rebel Alliance. The weapon was created with shipboard use in mind so it fires bolts that cannot breach the hull of a starship but can penetrate military-grade armor. Rebel soldiers are trained to practice safe firearms use, and the Alliance modifies all blaster pistols to include a safety that prevents accidental discharges. The DH-17 has a special feature in that it can be modified to fire in short bursts, which can be extremely useful in emergency situations. The modification is difficult to complete and has two major drawbacks: "Burst fire" drains the power pack in approximately 20 seconds and the excess heat generated by the bursts can melt the weapon's internal circuitry and cause an explosive overload. The weapon's sturdy construction enables use in hostile climates, such as on the ice planet Hoth, and a flash suppressor allows night concealment. The DH-17 is used extensively by the Rebel Alliance infantry forces.

54 Galven pattern damping sleeve
55 Rangefinder
56 Targeting sensor array
57 Power cell release
58 Photomultiplier
59 Scope settings adjust
60 Primary login processor
61 Image subprocessor
62 Electronic target display
63 Emitter nozzle

64 Flash suppressant matrix
65 Collimating ring
66 Galven circuitry
67 Static pulse adaptors
68 Prismatic focusing crystal
69 Actuating blaster module
70 Power cell magazine
71 APAS connectors
72 Trigger

73 Force-setting
74 Firing capac
75 Gas cell rele
76 Gas cell ac
77 Magnatomic adhesion gr

REBEL MARKSMEN

At the Battle of Hoth, veteran Rebel soldiers—including Alliance Special Forces (SpecForce) Wilderness Fighters and graduates of the Galactic Outdoor Survival School—fought shoulder-to-shoulder with fresh recruits in deep snow trenches to defend the Rebel evacuation against the Imperial assault on Echo Base. Mostly armed with BlasTech A280s, Rebel marksmen picked off white-armored snowtroopers and helped slow the enemy advance, but they soon became overwhelmed and were forced to retreat.

LONG RANGE SCOPE

The Novaless Soni-Optics Target Imager is a computerized scope that can be easily fitted to most blaster rifles. It uses a pair of ultrasonic beam emitters operating at different frequencies to sight on a target. As collectors receive the slightly different wave patterns from a target, a small data analyzer constructs a three-dimensional "sound pattern" that becomes visible through the scope. The sound pattern is unaffected by the level of light or heat present that might otherwise render more conventional sighting systems ineffective, thereby allowing the user to ignore certain types of cover and concealment.

BLASTECH A280 BLASTER

Although BlasTech Industries refuses to join the Empire and continues to supply weapons to the public sector, almost all military-grade BlasTech blaster rifles—such as the E-11—are manufactured for Imperial forces. Fortunately, disgruntled BlasTech employees and covert Rebel agents have obtained a large number of A280 blaster rifles. Based on the BlasTech DLT-20A, the A280 is distinguished from its predecessor by a slight bulge at its midsection. The bulge is the result of space requirements for the galven circuits, which are more bunched near the focusing crystals of the A280. This change increases the weapon's accuracy and stopping power. Heavier than the E-11, the A280 has a range of 300 meters (980 feet), can pierce stormtrooper armor at 150 meters (490 feet), and uses standard rechargeable power packs that have enough energy for fifty shots. The rifle's controls allow the shooter to alternate between semiautomatic, fully automatic, and pulse-fire settings. A280s require regular maintenance, but proper care ensures consistent reliability. Rebels used the A280 at the Battle of Hoth and the Battle of Endor.

18 Extendable buttstock
19 Electronic sight
80 Gas conversion enabler
81 Rangefinder
82 Ultrasonic beam emitter
83 Prismatic crystal housing

84 Integrated muzzle compensator
85 Magnatomic adhesion g
86 Power charge system
87 Power pack release
88 Power pack status indica

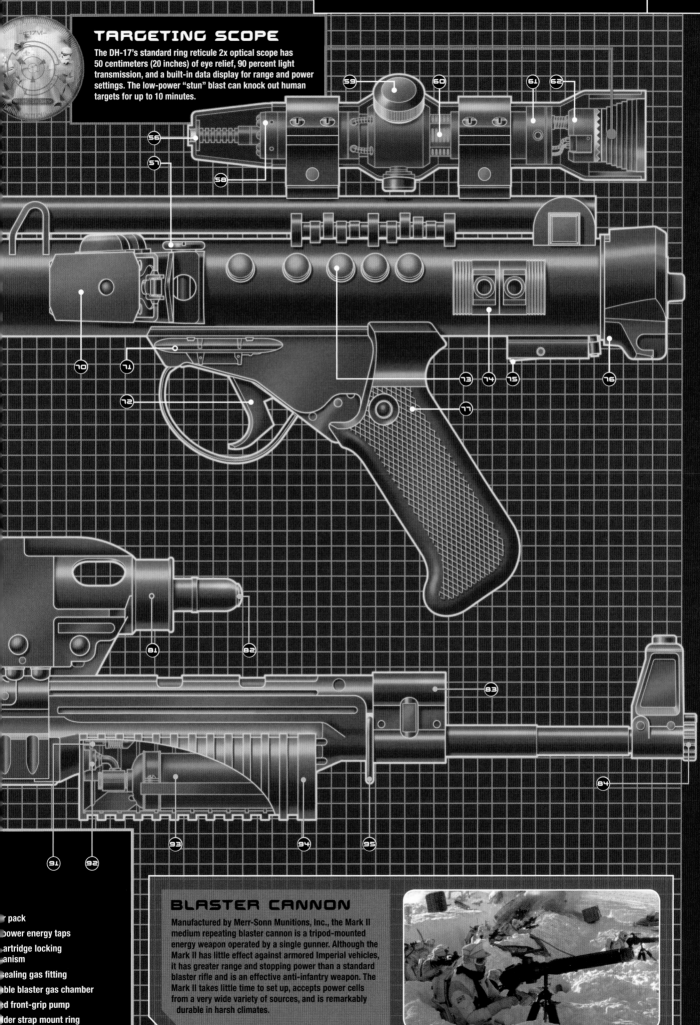

TARGETING SCOPE

The DH-17's standard ring reticule 2x optical scope has 50 centimeters (20 inches) of eye relief, 90 percent light transmission, and a built-in data display for range and power settings. The low-power "stun" blast can knock out human targets for up to 10 minutes.

BLASTER CANNON

Manufactured by Merr-Sonn Munitions, Inc., the Mark II medium repeating blaster cannon is a tripod-mounted energy weapon operated by a single gunner. Although the Mark II has little effect against armored Imperial vehicles, it has greater range and stopping power than a standard blaster rifle and is an effective anti-infantry weapon. The Mark II takes little time to set up, accepts power cells from a very wide variety of sources, and is remarkably durable in harsh climates.

pack
power energy taps
artridge locking
anism
ealing gas fitting
ble blaster gas chamber
d front-grip pump
der strap mount ring

Over the course of 18 months, Major Kem Monnon directed the Alliance Corps of Engineers to expand some of Hoth's existing caverns, move millions of tons of rock, and blast and carve ice walls into hangar areas, launch bays, command centers, barracks, medical centers, and interconnecting tunnels. Two more months were spent fitting Rebel electronics, weapons, life support, and maintenance gear. Completed just in time for the first wave of arriving starfighters, the vast underground complex designated Echo Base is merely a temporary facility, for Rebels know they cannot hide from the Empire indefinitely.

TAUNTAUNS

Because airspeeders and other repulsorlift vehicles cannot function in subzero temperatures without extensive modification, Rebels utilize tauntauns—Hoth's indigenous reptomammals—as mounts for patrol duties outside Echo Base. Han Solo rode a tauntaun on his mission to place life-form and motion sensors around the base's perimeter.

MEDICAL CENTER

Not surprisingly, most of the patients at Echo Base's medical center require treatment for cold-climate injuries such as frostbite, hypothermia, and snow blindness. But the local Hoth wildlife can be dangerous too. After a wampa ice monster mauled Luke Skywalker, the Industrial Automaton surgical droid 2-1B used flesh-regenerating bacta to treat the Rebel hero's injuries.

COMMAND CENTER

A dark, reinforced chamber filled with sophisticated machinery, Echo Base's command center is where General Rieekan issues orders to the Rebel troops. Communications specialists relay messages throughout the base while scanner operators monitor incoming data from the sensors placed by tauntaun-mounted scouts in the Hoth wilderness.

Echo Base

After the Battle of Yavin, the Rebel Alliance searched for a world to be a new secret base of operations. Although the ice planet Hoth—the fifth planet in the Hoth system in the Anoat sector—had previously been a refuge for smugglers and even a pair of Imperial-manufactured human replica droids before the unintentional arrival of Luke Skywalker and C-3PO, the desolate world was so remote that it was not on any standard navigational charts. Noting the ice caves that the defunct replica droids had used for shelter and the planet's far-flung location, Luke recommended Hoth as a possible Rebel base. Alliance brass agreed, and the result is one of the largest underground Rebel bases ever constructed. Designated Echo Base because of the strange acoustics of the interconnecting caves, the subterranean complex is protected by a small planetary shield.

BASE INTERIOR

Starfighter squadrons including X-wings and Y-wings are stored in Echo Base's hangar and launch areas. Groups of modified Incom T-47 airspeeders—dubbed "snowspeeders"— are launched at regular intervals for reconnaissance. Because the base's structural material is solid ice, freezing temperatures must be maintained to prevent meltdowns and devastating cave-ins. Walls of living quarters are covered with insulating plastic, allowing rooms to be heated to some degree of comfort. Massive, retractable doors are normally open during the day to allow passage for vehicles and scouts riding domesticated indigenous tauntauns, but are sealed at night to insulate personnel and equipment. Hangar 7, situated in the mouth of Echo Base's north end, holds X-wings as well as Han Solo's freighter, the *Millennium Falcon*.

1. North entrance blast door
2. Routing illuminators
3. Airspeeder bay
4. Ice-cutter
5. *Millennium Falcon*
6. Luke's X-wing
7. Starfighter pilots' ready room
8. North corridor
9. Elevator to maintenance level
10. Tauntaun pen
11. Tack room for tauntaun riders
12. Backup computers
13. Turbolift cluster
14. Vaccines storage
15. Central command and control room
16. Briefing chamber/ holoprojector room
17. South corridor
18. Mess hall
19. Medical center
20. Central forum
21. Intensive-care unit
22. Barracks
23. Rec room

MAIN HANGAR

Just inside the blast doors of Echo Base's main north entrance, Rebel mechanics and technicians work in grueling shifts with numerous droi to make sure that all X-wing starfighters and modified T-47 airspeeder are ready for combat or evacuation. Although various Rebels have offered to help with repairs and flight-preparation for the *Millennium Falcon*, Han Solo and his first mate, Chewbacca the Wookiee, prefer to work on their ship themselves.

R-75 MEDIUM TRANSPORT

...nufactured by Gallofree Yards and sold to ...Rebel Alliance at an incredible discount, ...90-meter (300-feet)-long GR-75 medium ...nsport is essentially an armored shell with ...argo capacity of 19,000 metric tons. Used ...transporting supplies, the GR-75 carries ...dreds of modular cargo pods, each with ...icated repulsorlift devices for rapid loading ...unloading. Although the largely vulnerable ...nsports require starfighter escorts during ...ckade runs, each has a rudimentary deflector ...eld system and four retractable twin laser ...nnons. Because of their role at the Battle of ...oth, GR-75s became generally known as "Rebel transports."

24 Principle reactor cowl

25 Primary drive engines (3)

26 Secondary drive engines (6)

27 Command pod

28 Landing gear (retracted)

29 Cargo modules

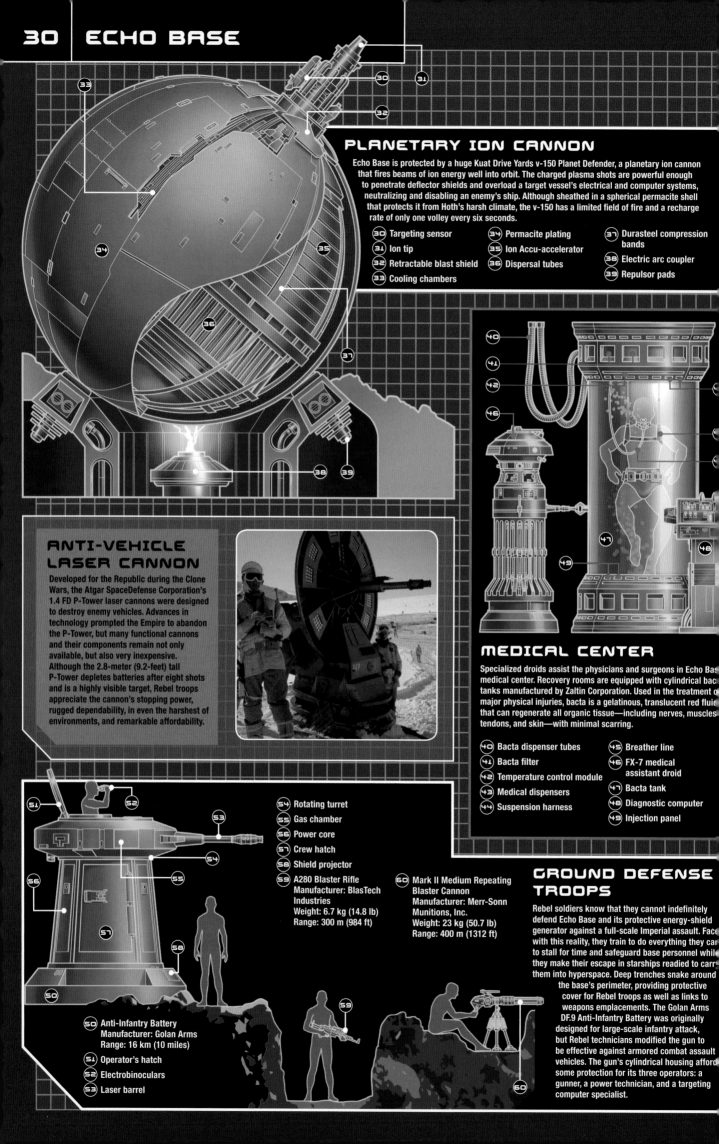

PLANETARY ION CANNON

Echo Base is protected by a huge Kuat Drive Yards v-150 Planet Defender, a planetary ion cannon that fires beams of ion energy well into orbit. The charged plasma shots are powerful enough to penetrate target vessel's deflector shields and overload a target vessel's electrical and computer systems, neutralizing and disabling an enemy's ship. Although sheathed in a spherical permacite shell that protects it from Hoth's harsh climate, the v-150 has a limited field of fire and a recharge rate of only one volley every six seconds.

30 Targeting sensor	34 Permacite plating	37 Durasteel compression bands
31 Ion tip	35 Ion Accu-accelerator	
32 Retractable blast shield	36 Dispersal tubes	38 Electric arc coupler
33 Cooling chambers		39 Repulsor pads

ANTI-VEHICLE LASER CANNON

Developed for the Republic during the Clone Wars, the Atgar SpaceDefense Corporation's 1.4 FD P-Tower laser cannons were designed to destroy enemy vehicles. Advances in technology prompted the Empire to abandon the P-Tower, but many functional cannons and their components remain not only available, but also very inexpensive. Although the 2.8-meter (9.2-feet) tall P-Tower depletes batteries after eight shots and is a highly visible target, Rebel troops appreciate the cannon's stopping power, rugged dependability, in even the harshest of environments, and remarkable affordability.

MEDICAL CENTER

Specialized droids assist the physicians and surgeons in Echo Base medical center. Recovery rooms are equipped with cylindrical bacta tanks manufactured by Zaltin Corporation. Used in the treatment of major physical injuries, bacta is a gelatinous, translucent red fluid that can regenerate all organic tissue—including nerves, muscles, tendons, and skin—with minimal scarring.

40 Bacta dispenser tubes	45 Breather line
41 Bacta filter	46 FX-7 medical assistant droid
42 Temperature control module	47 Bacta tank
43 Medical dispensers	48 Diagnostic computer
44 Suspension harness	49 Injection panel

54 Rotating turret	
55 Gas chamber	
56 Power core	
57 Crew hatch	
58 Shield projector	
59 A280 Blaster Rifle Manufacturer: BlasTech Industries Weight: 6.7 kg (14.8 lb) Range: 300 m (984 ft)	60 Mark II Medium Repeating Blaster Cannon Manufacturer: Merr-Sonn Munitions, Inc. Weight: 23 kg (50.7 lb) Range: 400 m (1312 ft)

50 Anti-Infantry Battery
Manufacturer: Golan Arms
Range: 16 km (10 miles)

51 Operator's hatch

52 Electrobinoculars

53 Laser barrel

GROUND DEFENSE TROOPS

Rebel soldiers know that they cannot indefinitely defend Echo Base and its protective energy-shield generator against a full-scale Imperial assault. Faced with this reality, they train to do everything they can to stall for time and safeguard base personnel while they make their escape in starships readied to carry them into hyperspace. Deep trenches snake around the base's perimeter, providing protective cover for Rebel troops as well as links to weapons emplacements. The Golan Arms DF.9 Anti-Infantry Battery was originally designed for large-scale infantry attack, but Rebel technicians modified the gun to be effective against armored combat assault vehicles. The gun's cylindrical housing affords some protection for its three operators: a gunner, a power technician, and a targeting computer specialist.

ICE MOUNTAIN HIDEOUT

...el scouts determined that the cavern-hollowed mountain in the ...thern Clabburn Range was suitable for a hidden fortress. Tall ...tilation shafts travel through several levels of ice and a series ...rbolifts provides access to defensive trenches on the planetary ...ace. Plasmold insulation and armored doors situated at the north ...ance and two southern entrances help to protect the base from ...'s sub-freezing temperatures and ice storms.

61	North Entrance	67	Medical center
62	Hangar 7	68	Fuel silo
63	Maintenance level	69	Transports hangar
64	Officers' quarters	70	South entrance control room
65	Turbolifts	71	South Entrance 1
66	Barracks	72	South Entrance 2

LASER ICE CUTTER

...nted to a vehicle or stationary tripod, the Corellian ...ineering Corporation's LC-10bW sheers through ...k ice with remarkable precision. The Rebel Alliance ...ps of Engineers used laser cutters along with ...avator machinery to expand caves, create grottoes, ...install connections between chambers. Despite ...r purpose, cutters need careful maintenance to ...d damage in sub-freezing temperatures.

- **Activator**
- **Laser guide**
- 75 **Barrel**
- 76 **Emitter nozzle**

WAMPA CONTAINMENT

**Lethal Hazard
DISMEMBERMENT**

Soon after the Rebels began construction of Echo Base, they encountered deadly wampa ice creatures: White-furred predators, virtually invisible against the snow and so well adapted at conserving heat that most life-form sensors fail to detect them. The Rebels trapped several wampa creatures in chambers sealed by strong, clearly marked doors. If stormtroopers arrive, C-3PO thinks the wampas should greet them.

POWER GENERATORS

...heavy-duty generators were too large and thermally ...nsive for underground installation, four immense ...erators were built outside Echo Base. They produce ...rgy for a planetary deflector shield strong enough ...eflect any orbital bombardment. Layers of insulation ...tect the fragile components from the deep cold.

77 **Temperature control coils**   78 **Modular power interconnect**

LONDON, NEW YORK, MUNICH
MELBOURNE AND DELHI

For Dorling Kindersley

Designer Jon Hall
Senior Designer Ron Stobbart
Senior Editor Elizabeth Dowsett
Managing Editor Catherine Saunders
Art Director Lisa Lanzarini
Category Publisher Simon Beecroft
Production Editor Marc Staples
Production Controller Nick Seston

For Lucasfilm

Executive Editor J. W. Rinzler
Art Director Troy Alders
Keeper of the Holocron Leland Chee
Director of Publishing Carol Roeder

First published in the United States in 2010
by DK Publishing
375 Hudson Street
New York, New York 10014

10 11 12   10 9 8 7 6 5 4 3 2 1

SD443—05/10

A catalog record for this book is available
from the Library of Congress.

ISBN: 978-0-7566-5203-6

Color reproduction by Media Development and Printing Ltd, UK.
Printed and bound in China by Leo Paper Products.

Discover more at
www.dk.com
www.starwars.com